Hey Jack!

The Scary Solo
first published in 2012
this edition published in 2017 by
Hardie Grant Egmont
Ground Floor, Building 1, 658 Church Street
Richmond, Victoria 3121, Australia
www.hardiegrantegmont.com.au

A CiP record for this title is available from the National Library of Australia

Text copyright © 2012 Sally Rippin
Illustration copyright © 2012 Stephanie Spartels
Logo and design copyright © 2012 Hardie Grant Egmont

Design by Stephanie Spartels
Typesetting by Michaela Stone

Printed in China through Asia Pacific Offset

1 3 5 4 2

Hey Jack!

The Scary Solo

By Sally Rippin
Illustrated by Stephanie Spartels

hardie grant EGMONT

Feels excited, but a little bit sick

Legs feel shaky

Jittery Mood

Chapter One

This is Jack.

This morning Jack is in a jittery mood. He wants to try for a solo in the school concert.

Jack likes singing,
but he feels too shy
to try out by himself.
So he has asked his
best friend Billie
to stand with him
while he sings.

Billie and Jack
practise singing in the
playground. They are
going to be **stars**!

2

'Next, please,' calls Miss Winters. She is in charge of the school concert. Today she is choosing children for the solo parts.

Now it is Jack's turn to try out for a part.

Jack walks onto the stage.

Billie follows and stands next to him.

Jack gets ready to sing.

But all of a sudden Jack feels nervous and wobbly. He hops from one foot to the other like he has **ants in his pants**.

The music starts. Jack
knows all the words
but when he opens his
mouth, nothing comes out!

Jack stands with his mouth
wide open. His tummy
squeezes tight.

Billie pokes him
in the ribs. 'Hey Jack!'
she says. 'What's wrong?'

Jack closes his mouth.
It's no use. He is much
too **scared**
to sing on his own.
He feels silly
for even trying.

Miss Winters smiles kindly. 'Perhaps you can be in the chorus, Jack. Now, Billie, are you trying out too?'

Billie nods. The music starts, and Billie sings loudly and clearly.

Jack feels cross and sad at the same time. He wishes he was as brave as Billie.

'Well done, Billie!'
says Miss Winters when
Billie has finished.
'You can have a solo.
You sing very well.'

Billie jumps up and
down in excitement.

Jack frowns. *But I can
sing, too!* he thinks crossly.
*I can sing as well as Billie!
It's just that…*

Jack sighs. He hangs his head as he and Billie leave the hall.

Chapter Two

Billie runs out into the playground. Jack mooches along behind her.

'I can't believe it!' says Billie. 'I got a solo!'

All the kids in the
playground stand
around Billie and
cheer for her.

Jack can see that Billie
is happy. He wants
to be happy too.
But right now he just
feels **cross**.

It was *his* idea to try out
for a solo in the school
concert. Not Billie's!

Jack scrunches up his
face and kicks the ground.

He feels a big dark
monster inside him
grumbling to be let out.

'It's only a stupid
school concert!'
Jack shouts. 'Who wants
to sing a solo anyway?
Only stupid people!'

Billie turns to Jack.
Her mouth drops open
and her eyes grow wide.

'Jack!' she says. 'That's
mean!'

Jack knows it's mean.
But he can't help it.
It's the big grumpy
monster talking, not him.

18

Jack runs away from Billie to the other end of the playground.

For the rest of the day, Jack and Billie don't speak to each other. Jack glares at Billie and she glares back.

Jack wants Billie to say sorry. He doesn't know why.

It's not fair that she got a solo in the school concert and he didn't.

But soon the **grumpy** monster in Jack's tummy goes away. He knows it is up to him to say sorry.

'I'm sorry for being mean,' he says. 'I'm happy that you got a solo, Billie. Really. Friends?'

'Friends,' Billie says, smiling. 'Forever.'

21

'Hey, maybe you can help me practise my solo?' Billie adds.

Jack nods. 'Sure,' he says. 'I'd like that.'

All that week and the next, Jack helps Billie practise her solo for the musical.

They sing everywhere. In the kitchen and in the bathroom. In the garden and in the house.

24

They sing as loud as
rock stars – except when
it's time for Billie's
baby brother to have
a nap. Then they sing
baby Noah to sleep.

Jack can't wait for
the concert!

Chapter Three

Finally the day of
the school concert
arrives. Jack and Billie's
families drive to the
school hall.

Billie and Jack are both wearing shiny silver tops. This is the costume their class is wearing for the concert.

Billie also has glitter in her hair. She looks just like a rock star.

Jack feels a teensy bit **jealous** when he sees Billie's hair. He wishes he had a solo, too. He knows being in the chorus is an important job, but it's not as exciting as being a solo singer.

'Good luck, Billie!'
their parents shout
excitedly. 'Hey Jack!
Good luck!'

Billie and Jack
wave to their
parents. They
run back stage.
Jack skips
with excitement.

Soon it's time for
the concert to begin.

Every class is doing
a different song in
the concert. Jack and
Billie wait with their
class until it is their
turn to go on stage.

They wait and they wait.
Everyone is nervous
and **giggly**.

Sometimes Miss Winters
pokes her head into the
back room and frowns.

'Shhh!' she says
with her finger on
her lips. But this
just makes everyone
giggle even more.

Jack and Billie
practise their song
very quietly together.

Only two more songs
and they are on!

Jack feels his tummy
flipping like a fish.

'OK!' Miss Winters whispers to Jack's class. 'You're up next!'

Everyone in Jack's class runs onto the stage and stands in their positions. Billie stands in front, ready to sing her solo.

'Go, Billie!' Jack whispers.

The curtains open.

The music starts.

The spotlight shines
on Billie. Everyone
waits for her to sing.

Billie lifts up her
microphone. Her
mouth opens. But no
sound comes out!

Oh no! Jack thinks.

35

He knows *exactly*
what's wrong with Billie.
He knows that her legs
will be **wobbling**
like jelly.

The music stops.
Everybody looks at Billie,
waiting… waiting…

Poor Billie! thinks Jack.
She has no-one to help her!

Billie is still standing
at the front, frozen.

Wait a second, thinks Jack.
I know this solo!

He runs to stand
next to Billie. Then he
grabs the microphone
and holds it between
himself and Billie.
He begins to sing.

The music starts
up again. Jack sings
loud and strong.
He knows all the words
off by heart.

Billie stands with
her eyes wide open.

Still singing, Jack
jabs her with
his elbow. He looks
at her and smiles.

Finally she starts
to sing too. Quietly
at first, but then
louder and louder.

Soon Jack and
Billie are singing
at the top of
their voices.
Just like at home.

When Jack and
Billie's class has
finished the song,
everyone claps
and cheers.

People **stomp**
their feet on the ground
and shout, 'More! More!'

Jack and Billie's
parents cheer the
loudest of all.

Jack's smile stretches
across his face.
He looks at all those
cheering people.

41

He feels a big warm
burst of sunshine
in his chest.

He is a star!

43

Hey Jack! The Crazy Cousins By Sally Rippin

Hey Jack! The Scary Solo By Sally Rippin

Hey Jack! The Winning Goal By Sally Rippin

Hey Jack! The Robot Blues By Sally Rippin

Hey Jack! The Worry Monsters By Sally Rippin

Hey Jack! The New Friend By Sally Rippin

Hey Jack! The Worst Sleepover By Sally Rippin

Hey Jack! The Lost Reindeer By Sally Rippin

Hey Jack! The Circus Lesson By Sally Rippin

Hey Jack! The Bumpy Ride By Sally Rippin

Hey Jack! The Top Team By Sally Rippin

Hey Jack! The Playground Problem By Sally Rippin

Hey Jack! The Best Party Ever By Sally Rippin

Hey Jack! The Big Adventure By Sally Rippin

Hey Jack! The Bravest Kid By Sally Rippin

Hey Jack! The Toy Sale By Sally Rippin

Hey Jack! The Other Teacher By Sally Rippin

Hey Jack! The Party Invite By Sally Rippin

Hey Jack! The Extra-special Group By Sally Rippin

Hey Jack! The Star of the Week By Sally Rippin